The Test

ALSO BY SYLVAIN NEUVEL

THE TEST

SYLVAIN NEUVEL

A TOM DOHERTY ASSOCIATES BOOK

NEW YORK

THE TEST

Cover design by Jonathan Gray

Edited by Lee Harris

A Tor.com Book
Published by Tom Doherty Associates
175 Fifth Avenue
New York, NY 10010
www.tor.com

Tor® is a registered trademark of
Macmillan Publishing Group, LLC.

ISBN 978-1-250-31282-2 (ebook)
ISBN 978-1-250-31283-9 (trade paperback)

First Edition: February 2019

To kind people

The Test

1.

The Life in the United Kingdom Test

QUESTION 1: WHO IS THE PATRON SAINT OF WALES
AND ON WHICH DATE IS HIS FEAST DAY?

I know the answer! It's Saint David, on March first. I met Tidir, my wife, on March first. It is our meeting anniversary. I remember that day. She came in for a root canal and I fell in love. Not with her— I didn't know who she was and she didn't exactly talk a lot with the mouth prop on. I fell in love with her teeth. She had striped canines. Horizontal discolouration of the enamel, right down the middle. Her teeth look like Neapolitan ice cream. Neapolitan cuspids. I knew right away.

We met again in a café weeks later. I asked if I could sit with her, and she said yes. A month later, we were married. If you ask her why she married me, she'll say she was in pain before she met me and I made it go away. I did fix her tooth. The rest of it runs deeper than I can reach.

She's been through a lot. It's for her that we had to leave.

We celebrate our meeting day more than we do our wedding anniversary. We both *chose* to get married, but that root canal, that was the will of Allah. I decorate the house, cover the kitchen floor with rose petals. Sometimes I use tulips, but I don't tell her. I make my Fesenjān, if I can find nice pomegranates. Our first year in London, our neighbour asked if we were celebrating Saint David's day. He's from Wales. I think that was supposed to be a joke, but we have been best friends ever since. Now we celebrate together. Fesenjān and Welsh rarebit. This question is a sign. This is going to be a *great* day!

It didn't start so well. They gave me a physical when we first arrived. I hate physicals. I have no problem with needles if I'm the one holding the syringe, but I get queasy staring at the receiving end. It was over quickly, though, and then they took us here. Wow. You say immigration office and I think grey building, bad lighting, yellowed walls. I imagined taking the test on an old school desk with chewed pieces of gum underneath. This place feels like a fancy hotel. Gorgeous lobby. Absolutely gorgeous. Old meets new, stainless steel and mahogany. They had the same paper slippers we used at my practice in Teheran. Tidir doesn't like those, but I do. I like the feel of the floor on my toes. It was still early and we all got a fresh pair from the clean pile.

There was an Asian man screaming at the receptionist when we walked in. He called her a racist, kept saying she stole money from him, gave him less change than what he was owed. I told him he was being impolite and sent him on his way. He may have been right, about the change that is. When I paid the fifty pound fee for the test, the receptionist gave me back a twenty pound note instead of a ten. I had to explain her mistake to her twice before she took it back. I almost told her it was a tip. I didn't. These people have no sense of humour whatsoever. It must be a requirement for working at Immigration. Hello! My name is Idir Jalil, this is my wife Tidir. . . . Nothing. Not even a smile. Idir and Tidir. That usually gets us a chuckle, at least. Not here. I did not give up. You can change the world with one smile. Do you know the difference between a customs officer and a dentist? There isn't one. They both do cavity searches. No sense of humour, I tell you. There was a redheaded man in the waiting room who made a crude joke about the receptionist's cleavage. His joke wasn't funny, but I have a lot of good dentist jokes. What does the dentist of the year get? A little plaque. . . . They showed me to the test room.

What a room! Wooden desks with fancy data pads. The chair . . . this chair is more comfortable than any chair I have ever sat in. It is decided. After the test I will find out where they purchased it and I will get that chair for myself. The room is small—there are only four desks—but there are windows all around and it feels very open. I can see Tidir in the waiting room. I can see my son, Ramzi, and my daughter, Salma. It was nice of them to come. My wife said it was the least they could do since I am the only one taking the test. Only men. Only between the ages of sixteen and forty-five. She said it was unfair. I told her it was a blessing. I do not care what their motivations are; it is a simple matter of probabilities. I heard that one in three people fails the test. If that is true and I alone am required to pass, our family has a sixty-six percent chance at citizenship. If two of us are tested, then the odds go down to forty-three percent. She said I was naive. I do not see what is naive about mathematics. The world is what you make of it, I told her. She smiled.

QUESTION 2: A LOT OF PEOPLE CARVE LANTERNS OUT OF _____ AND PUT A CANDLE INSIDE OF THEM DURING HALLOWEEN.

Ramzi would like this question. He loves Halloween. That is probably his favourite thing about England. He starts talking about his costume months in advance, as early as July. He'll change his mind a dozen times and we always end up making it at the last minute. He was a space pirate last year. Ramzi was one year old when we left Teheran, so he doesn't remember, but we did have Halloween in Iran. We'd walk by houses and hear music in the basement, see someone wearing a mask through the window. Teenagers, always. Too brazen to fear the Basij, too young to realize how much they should. People have been accused of witchcraft, satanism for merely attending such parties. We never saw any pumpkins, though. Ramzi asks us for one every year. We said yes and bought one, once, made pumpkin pie with the insides. We hated it, all of us. We make costumes for the children, but we do not buy pumpkins anymore. It feels wrong to waste a beautiful giant fruit. It is a fruit, is it not? It has seeds. . . . Things with seeds are—

—*How long do we have?*

What? My test neighbour is talking to me. I am fairly certain we are not allowed to talk, mister. I wore a base-ball cap for my citizenship test. Then again, this is the same man who came through the door exactly as I was walking in and pushed me aside. I shouldn't be too sur-prised. I will not answer him.

—*For the test. How long do we have?*

Please stop talking, mister. It says right at the top. You have forty-five minutes to complete the test.

—*Do* you *know?*

Fine! I will tell you.

—We have forty-five minutes.

There. I said it. Now stop talking before—

—Sir. There is no talking during the test.

That voice came through the speakers. But he— No, I will not get upset. He is just nervous. He is. His leg is shaking. If I were unsure about how long we have, I would also want to know. Now I have told him and he feels better. That is well worth being scolded by the attendant. Life is what you make of it. This is a good day.

QUESTION 3: TAKING PUBLIC TRANSPORTATION IS GOOD FOR THE ENVIRONMENT. TRUE OR FALSE?

A city question. People who talk a lot about the environment are always the ones living the farthest away from nature. True. Public transportation is indeed better than driving. . . . That is what they mean. It must be. That question is poorly worded. How could no one have noticed that? Walking is a lot better for the environment than public transportation, and so is riding a bicycle. Perhaps this is a new question. Deep breath. Stop overthinking, Idir. The answer is true.

Tidir and I do not own a car. Neither of us likes to drive. I wish I could say we walk everywhere to save the planet, but the truth is we are both horrible drivers.

People keep telling me how bad the air is in London. Worse than Beijing, they say. I tell them they should be happy it still looks like air. In Teheran, we spent the better part of winter cutting through brown haze, thick dark clouds of sulphur dioxide—lots of things that end in -xide—asbestos, even rubber. Who wants to breathe in rubber? They say it is because the gasoline is so bad. I doubt there is asbestos in gasoline.

QUESTION 4: KING RICHARD III OF THE HOUSE OF YORK WAS KILLED IN THE BATTLE OF BOSWORTH FIELD IN WHAT YEAR?

I should leave a note for question 3. Hmmm, there is no room for notes. It is fine. It is fine. The Battle of Bosworth Field was fought in . . . 1485. I am positive. That is the answer. I wonder who writes these questions. How will knowing this make me a better member of British society? We have been living in London for five years. My son has no memory of Iran and my daughter was born here. We have been asked why we hate freedom, told to go back to the desert many times—I tell them I hear Dasht-e Kavir is breathtaking but I have never been. It is true—but not once has anyone asked me about famous battles of the fifteenth century. Maybe I should bring it up.

I have a feeling only the people taking this test know the answer to that question. What could anyone *possibly* do with that information? It would have come in handy in, say, 1485, if one were travelling the country. Darling, perhaps Bosworth Field is not the best spot for a picnic today. The horses are fine. I think we should keep trotting. I should not—

Seriously? Mr. Baseball Cap spilled his coffee on his desk. No reaction. He is just sitting there, looking at the mess. Do something!... Stop judging, Idir. Get up and help the man... There are to be some napkins near the coffee machine. Where are they? There. That should be enough.

—*Here you go, sir. Let me help you.*

—*Oh, thanks. I'm just... really nervous.*

Why was I so quick to judge this man? I must be nervous, myself. There is a lesson to be learned here. We are all more alike than we think.

QUESTION 5: THE "GUNNERS" IS THE NICKNAME OF WHICH PREMIER LEAGUE FOOTBALL CLUB?

Finally, something useful.

They should make this whole test about football. Sports bring people together like nothing else. It might be even truer here than it was in Teheran. Our neighbour took me to the pub a few weeks after we met. I was hesitant at first. A lot of Iranians will drink alcohol—we did on occasion—but doing it in public does not come naturally. I figured the people who would object were not likely to be in a pub, and I said yes. I loved the ambiance. People singing and cheering. We were standing near the bar watching the Arsenal. I don't remember who they were playing. I was too self-conscious to openly celebrate, but when the Gunners scored, this hulking giant of man grabbed me by the shoulders and squeezed me like a sponge. It was the first time I felt like I belonged, like I was truly welcome. There have been other times since, many of them, but there was something special about that game.

I wish— What was that noise? It sounded like a gunshot. That *was* a gunshot. Most people don't know what a gunshot sounds like. It sounds like a garbage container being closed hard, like someone popping a plastic bag, anything but a gunshot. Most people don't know that, until they do. Then it is impossible not to recognize it. Why would anyone fire a gun at the immigration office?

Oh. There are . . . four, no, five men coming in; I can see them through the window—large men. They are all wearing ski masks—black, black combat fatigues. They have tactical vests. And guns. They have . . . lots of guns, automatic weapons. Are they soldiers? They look *exactly* like the IRGC forces in Iran, the Islamic Revolutionary Guard. All black. Daunting. I suppose they look exactly like *any* special forces. They could be British, SAS perhaps. This could be some sort of exercise? I hope—They are entering the waiting room. My family!

Everyone is getting on their knees. TIDIR! NO! DO NOT GET NEAR MY CHILDREN! Please, Tidir, do as they say. This is not an exercise. No. No. No. NO! How is this happening? Tidir . . . Tidir will be okay. She knows what to do. Stay silent. Don't draw attention to yourself.

One of them is coming this way. He's entering the test room.

—*Everyone! On your knees! Now!*

I am! I am on my knees. I have been here before. I have been thrown to the ground and I have felt the tip of their guns on the back of my neck. I have been through this and I have survived. We will survive. All of us. Someone will come. Someone will come and save us all.

—*I said now!*

What? Who isn't complying? Come on, Mr. Baseball Cap, do what he says! You will get yourself killed! You'll get someone else killed! No! Don't talk to them!

—*What is this? What do you want with us? We don't—*

That sound again, only much louder. They shot him!

Vay Khoda, they shot him! A loud thump. Mr. Baseball Cap is falling to the ground. Everyone is screaming. What should I do? Should I look? I have to look, raise my head slowly. No sudden movement. That is what they told me in Teheran. He's holding his leg. The dark stain on the wooden floor is growing rapidly. If they hit the artery, he will bleed out in minutes. Someone has to help him or he'll die.

Everyone has stopped screaming. Everyone but him. I will need something to stop the bleeding. My shirt. I can untie my shirt now, while I'm kneeling. Maybe someone else will— Maybe they— What am I thinking? That man will not help, he's the one who shot him. I'm the only one who can help. I *am* taking off my shirt. I'll stay close to the ground with my head down. There is so much blood. Mr. Baseball Cap is looking at me. I see so many emotions. Pain. Fear. I don't want to die. Distress. Please help me. Despair. I will do what I can.

—*Hey! You! What are you doing?*

—*Please don't shoot! Please! I'm just going to tie this around his leg. . . . There. That's it. It's done.*

—*Get back over there!*

I fear my heart will burst out of my chest. Look at the floor, Idir. Move away from him and keep looking at the floor. I hope he lives. He'll need medical attention soon. A real tourniquet would give him time. This, my shirt, it's not tight enough. It will slow the bleeding down a bit, but not much. I can't say for certain, but my guess is he has minutes, not hours. But he *is* alive for now. That is what matters. I'm alive. Tidir is alive. My children are alive.

2.

THIS CAN'T BE HAPPENING to us, not again. This is what we ran away from. Guns and impunity. This is why we're here. Men with guns knocking at the door in the middle of the night. Kneeling. Always kneeling. Watching her leave, not knowing if she was coming back. Ramzi crying for his mother, too young to understand why he gets a plastic bottle instead of a breast. Mommy will be back soon. She always came back. Always with the same look on her face. Resilience. She never talked about what they did to her. There was nothing to gain, a lot to lose. She didn't want it to change the way I looked at her. Tidir was a journalist, and a good one at that. Some pain came with the territory, but she felt guilty for making us share it. There are days when I regret not getting her to stop, not even trying. Not many, but some. Now she's kneeling again. She's calm. She knows this. She'll do what she needs to do to protect our children.

—*Everyone! It seems we have a good Samaritan among us.*

That voice is coming from across the window. It's

louder than before. I could not make out what anyone was saying a moment ago.

—*You! Samaritan! Look at me!*

He's banging on the window. Is he talking to me? Don't draw attention to yourself. That is what they told me. He *is* talking to me, standing behind the glass to my left. No one else is speaking. Deference. He must be the man in charge. He is smaller than the rest of them. There is a holstered pistol on his belt, nothing in his hands. Everyone else is holding a weapon.

—*I said look at me!*

I am looking at him, but I can't hold his stare. I have to say something. He singled me out because I helped the man in the baseball cap. He saw defiance. I put my head down again. Submission.

—*I just . . . I tried to stop the bleeding.*

That was a mistake. I shouldn't talk. I should do nothing.

—*Do I look shy?*

What? Don't answer that. Nothing good can come of this.

—*I asked you a question, Samaritan. Do I look shy to you?*

—*I'm sorry. I don't—*

—*Timid! Shy! Insecure! It's a simple question. DO. I. LOOK. SHY?*

It's a trap. I know. He knows that I know. He also knows I have no choice but to walk into it. He is testing me.

—*No, sir. I'm sorry.*

—*You're sorry that I don't look shy? Never mind that. Are you in control?*

—*In control?*

He wants me to panic. I can't.

—*Of this situation. Are you in control here? Are you in charge?*

—*No, sir.*

—*Then who is?*

—*You are, sir. You're in charge.*

He is the man in charge. He wanted me to know.

—*Then if I'm in control, and I don't, as you said, look timid or insecure, don't you think I would have asked if I wanted you to stop the bleeding? You, my friend, are meddling in shit that doesn't concern you.*

—*I'm not.*

Defiance. Stop it, Idir.

—*Like hell you're not!*

—*I won't do anything else, sir, I promise.*

—*Oh, but you will. You will if I tell you to! See, you chose to help that man. You made a decision. It wasn't yours to make and you know it. I know you do, you look like an intelligent man.*

—*I*—

—*Don't interrupt me, Samaritan! You even said it! "You are, sir. You're in charge." That tells me you understand the hierarchy. And yet! And yet, you made that decision* for *me.*

Have I done this? Have I gotten myself here? There's nothing I can say, no good answer. I might die today, and I don't know if it was inevitable or if I inched myself into it, one small mistake after the other. Don't draw attention to yourself. That is what they told me. It's too late for that. My head is spinning, thoughts going through my mind faster than I can catch them.

There's a television set in the waiting room behind the man in charge. No sound. I can't hear it through the window if there is. I see the building we're in. It's a helicopter shot. Dozens of police cars. Tactical teams. We must be on every channel. I can't read the text at the bottom of the screen. Tidir is still on her knees facing the floor; so are the kids. Good. She must know he's talking to me. I hope she doesn't do anything. She won't. She's smarter than I am. I bet she could read the small print if she were in this room. Tidir has the best eyesight. She can read street signs before I even know there is a street sign. She finds even the smallest toy parts Ramzi leaves behind. More aerial shots of the building. "Terrorism" in bold white letters, big enough even for me to see. I hope no one dies because of me. I've started a chain of events I can't seem to stop. Please let no one else suffer for it.

—*I tell you what, Samaritan. I have a phone call to make, but I'll get back to you in a sec. Don't worry.*

I *am* worried, but it feels good to have his eyes off me. He must be talking to the police. I can't hear the words, but he's probably making demands. It does not matter at this point. Either they'll surrender—that seems unlikely—or tactical teams will storm in and fire at everything that moves. People will get shot. Bad people, good people. Collateral damage. One thing is for sure, they will not meet their demands. They *will* negotiate—that could last for days—get the man in charge to release a few hostages if they can. That is what we are, now. Hostages. They will show good will, send some food, but in the end they will come in and people will die. I think I just heard him say "fifteen minutes."

—*Every fifteen minutes! You hear me!*

I do. I wonder if he was shouting to the people on the phone or if this was for our benefit. If it was, it seems pointless. Everyone here is already as scared as they can be. He's established his dominance; now what? All I can do is wait. There is no way out of this room, only the door I came in through. Even if there were, I could not leave without my family and the man in charge is standing five feet away from them. He is in control.

—*Samaritan! I told you I wouldn't forget about you!*

What does he want with me?

—*Samaritan! Look at me when I'm talking to you! What are you here for? Why are you in this room? Did they punish you because you stuck your nose where it didn't belong like you did with me?*

Maybe I can do some good. Maybe if he focuses all his attention on me, everyone else will be safe. My family will be safe.

—*I didn't. I'm . . . I'm here for a test.*

—*A test?! What kind of test?*

—*Ci . . . A citizenship test.*

—*Citizenship! That's right! You're a fucking immigrant! Where are you from?*

This is my chance. I cannot fade into the background anymore, but I can try to become human again. Right now, I am only a hostage to him, a means to an end. Dehumanized. If I share some personal things . . .

—*Teheran.*

—*You're from Irak!*

—*Iran.*

—*Iran, Irak . . . You're a Muslim, aren't you? Why'd you come here?*

—*We were . . . Our lives were in danger.*

—*Our lives . . . You have a family?*

—*Yes, sir. They came with me.*

—*Let me get this straight. You leave your country*

because ... *you're in danger. You take your wife, your kids? Kids, plural?*

—*Yes, sir. Two of them.*

—*Good for you. You get them out of Iran and you come to* this place, *and now you're here, today, for a fucking citizenship test. Wow. That's messed up. That is some* bad *fucking luck, my friend! How's it going?*

—*What?*

—*The test. How is it going so far?*

—*I ...*

—*Is it easy? Is it hard? Come on, Samaritan! I've got time. Let's get you through that test!*

—*...*

I don't know why is he's doing this. There's nothing genuine about him, nothing good.

—*I'm trying to help you here! Are you going to refuse my help?*

It does not matter why he is doing it. He is not hurting anyone while he's talking to me.

—*No, sir. Thank you, sir.*

—*There. Gratitude. That's what I like to hear. What's the next question?*

—*I ... It's on the desk, sir.*

—*Then get the fuck up and go back to your desk! We don't have all day!*

He had that man shot because he wouldn't get down.

Now he wants me to get up. Do what he says, Idir. Everything will be fine. I will not sit on the chair. I'll just kneel in front of the desk and swipe left to the next screen.

—*Yes, sir. It's . . . I'm at question six.*

—*Six! How many are there?*

—*Twenty-five. This is question six of twenty-five.*

—*Shit. That's a lot. We better hurry then. What's the question?*

—*How old was Mary Stuart when she became Queen of Scotland?*

—*That's the question?*

—*Yes, sir.*

—*What kind of question is that? Why do you need to know that to be a citizen? I don't know that!*

—*There are lots of historical questions, sir.*

—*And?*

—*That is the question, sir. How old was Mary Stuart when she became Queen of Scotland?*

—*What's the fucking answer?*

—*Oh. I don't know.*

I am much too scared to think, but I really don't know the answer. If I did, I might not have told him. I don't think I should. The last thing I want is to sound like a know-it-all.

—*You don't know?*

—*No, sir. I don't.*

—*Is it multiple choice or open answer?*

—*Multiple choice.*

—*Shoot!*

—*There are four . . . four answers to choose from: One week old. One month old. One year old. Five years old.*

—*None of these make sense. Does anyone know? Anyone?*

Please let no one answer. Please. Keep him focused on me.

—*People! Wake the fuck up! Samaritan here is going to flunk his test if no one answers!*

—*Six days. She was six days old.*

Who said that? It came from inside the test room. One of his men behind me.

—*Six days old! Are you sure?*

—*Uh-huh.*

—*Look at you, smarty-pants! That makes no sense, though. Six days old . . . What would she do? There ya go, lads! The baby pooped! Let's sack York!*

Does he expect us to laugh at his jokes? Let him speak, Idir. Let him speak all he wants. The longer this takes, the better chance we have. The police might come in.

—*All right, Samaritan, one down. What's the next one?*

—*Question seven. Which . . . Which stories are associated with—*

—*Oh oh! I'm afraid we're out of time, Samaritan. . . . Get up.*

—*What?*

—*Get up! I help you, now you help me. That's how it works. . . . I said get up! Good, come here.*

We are standing two feet from each other, only a window between us. He's staring at me. I won't stare back. I'll keep looking at the floor. For a second, I saw . . . There's something wrong about the way he looked at me. There's no . . . emotion, nothing in his eyes. I think I made a mistake. Humanizing myself won't change a thing. That man is a psychopath. He could not care less if I'm a person or not.

—*You! Get up. Over here.*

Who is he talking to? He's not looking at me anymore, the man in charge. He's helping someone off the floor. The redheaded man, I've seen him before. He was sitting in the corner when we came into the waiting room. He made that crude joke about the receptionist. He's wearing a suit, probably his one suit. I did not notice before, but it's a size too small and his shoes are worn. He looks about my age, maybe a bit older. Late forties.

—*Who do we have behind door number one? What's your name, sir? Oh, don't be shy.*

—*Graham.*

—*You can look up, everyone.*

He wants all of us to see this, whatever *this* is.

—*And what do you do for a living, Graham?*

—*I'm* ...

—*There's no crying at this game, Graham. Just tell me what you do.*

—*I'm an accountant.*

—*Sorry about that, Graham. But all right. Aaaand* ... *you. Fatty. Get up.*

That kid looks so scared. He's not a kid, he must be in his late twenties, but he looks ... pink skin, a little round. Soft, mostly. He's wearing a powder blue sweater, cashmere maybe. Looks expensive.

—*And what's your name, fat boy?*

—*...*

—*What is it with the crying?! I'm sorry, I didn't mean that. You're not fat, you're just* ... *What the fuck is your name, kid?*

—*Andrew. Andrew Shaw.*

—*And how do you spend your days, Andrew Andrew Shaw?*

—*I make ... I make designer—*

—*Never mind. I don't wanna know. ... Samaritan! Are you ready?*

He's rubbing his hands. He's proud of himself. I don't know where this is going, but I want it to end.

—*Ready for what? What do you want from me?*

—*I'm glad you asked* ... *I was on the phone a little while ago with the powers that be, and I asked them for* ... *things.*

Different things. They didn't like that, my asking for things. That's understandable. I hate it, too, when people ask. Call me lazy, but I don't like doing things, in general. I hate taking out the garbage, but I do. I do it because my whole flat will stink if I don't. I don't particularly like to eat. It's a shame, I know, but I don't. Obviously, I have to. I don't like stopping at red lights, but I do—I'm a very safe driver—because the police will stop me if I don't. You understand what I'm saying? I need motivation to do things.

The man in the blue sweater wants to get back on the floor.

—No! No! No! Get your—I was gonna say fat again, sorry. Get your ass back up, Andrew Andrew Shaw. This is for your benefit, too. Where was I? Oh, yes. The police, the government, they also need motivation to do things, so . . . I provided some. I told them that I would kill one person every fifteen minutes if I they didn't do what I asked them to do . . . Oh, and it's been fifteen minutes. And they didn't do what I asked them to do.

—Please don't do that. Please—

That's why he picked me. He wants to kill me in front of everyone! I don't want to die. Not like this, not in front of my children.

—Samaritan! I'm not gonna kill you! Look at you, all shaky and shit! What kind of asshole would I be, helping you with that test, if I put a bullet in your head halfway through?

No, I'm not gonna kill you. I'm gonna kill who you tell me to!

I don't know what he's saying. There has to be a way to stop this.

—*You don't need to kill anyone, sir. There's no need for that. I can talk to them, tell them—*

—*Tell them what? That I'm going to kill someone? I already told them that. Are you someone important? Do you think you're more important than me?*

—*No, sir. I'm not. I don't.*

—*That's what I thought. Now who'll it be?*

—*Be what? I don't understand.*

—*Who. Do. You. Want. Me. To. Kill? Do you have a hearing problem, Samaritan?*

—*I—No. I don't want you to kill anyone.*

—*Sure you do! You wanted to make decisions for me—you didn't think I forgot about that, did you?—well, now's your chance. You can either pick Graham, the accountant—*

—*No, not me! Please, sir!*

The redhead. He wants to kill the redhead.

—*Shut the fuck up, Graham. Or Andrew Andrew Shaw and his designer shit. Your choice.*

He wants to kill the redhead or the kid. I don't know what he expects from me. I won't do what he asks.

—*I won't do that. I won't choose.*

—*Goddamn it, Samaritan! THERE ARE RULES!*

Tell me what the rules are.

—I ...

—The rules! Oh, you haven't heard the rules yet, have you? My fault! I apologize. It's just—there's a lot going through my mind right now. You know how it is. Anyway, here are the rules. Every fifteen minutes, I pick two people and you tell me which one to kill. I kill that person. Simple enough!

—I told you. I won't do that. I'll do everything you want, but not that.

—Oh, come on! I'm doing the hard part. I'm the one with the gun. We can switch if you want, but I tell you: I'd rather be in your shoes. You just pick someone. It's a simple thing. Door number one, or door number two. That's it! You just tell me who to kill, and I do it ... OR ... I forgot about that part. It's kind of important. OR, I kill them both. ... See! You're saving someone, really. ... Who'll it be? Older guy with boring job, or fatty here with really bad taste in clothes. Is that fucking cashmere?

—I won't choose.

—Why?

—I can't. I can't tell you to kill someone.

—What do you mean, you can't? You can't just now, or like ever?

—Yes.

—Yes, ever? Like on principle?

—*Yes.*

—*That's bullshit! Like, if someone's holding a gun and he'll kill two people unless I tell him to kill one of them I won't do it? That's not a principle. That's just . . . some shit you came up with right now. Come on! Stop wasting my time.*

—*I'm sorry, sir. I*—

—*Now you're just pissing me off. I'm going to make this easy on you, Samaritan. I'm going to count to three, then I'll pull the trigger if I don't have an answer. Did you get that? One, two, three, then they die.*

—*No, I*—

—*Here we go. One.*

The hostages are looking at me, not him. I can't look at them. They look at me like I'm really deciding which one of them will live. I'm not. I can't help them. He's in control, not me. He's taunting me, messing with my head. He just wants to know if I'll do it or not. I won't. I'm not a killer. I won't make that choice.

—*TWO!*

He won't do it. He won't. . . . Even if he does, even if he kills them both. That's him, not me. I'm not responsible for this. It's his choice. Not mine. *He* wants to kill people. I choose love. I choose life.

—*Three. Did I say on three? Oh, fuck it.*

Don't d—

TAK

TAK

—NOOOOOO!!!!

The sound of bodies hitting the floor. I can't look.

3.

DOZENS OF COMPUTER SCREENS light up the control room. In the back, behind a glass wall, four people are sitting at their stations, viewing 3D scans of Idir's family and mapping their faces onto mesh bodies. In the centre, two people—a woman and a man—are sitting at a desk. Both are staring at a large screen showing Idir crawling on the floor, tying his shirt around the injured man's leg. On a smaller screen to the left, Idir is lying in what looks like a hospital bed, immobile. There are electrodes on both his temples. His eyes are closed and his eyelids are twitching.

The woman is white, early fifties. Her name is Laura. She wears a government-issued grey jumpsuit. She looks at the screen, unfazed by what she sees, and takes some notes on her data pad. This isn't new to her; she's overseen more than a hundred of these simulations. The job has taken its toll on her, but she still takes some pride in it. Only a handful of government employees can administer the BVA—the British Values Assessment.

The man is much younger, about half her age. His name is Deep. First in his family to be born in the UK, he picked up some of his parent's Indian accent but hides it very well. Deep isn't nearly as calm as his supervisor. This is his final evaluation, his last day as a trainee. First-generation citizens don't often get this job, and Deep is well aware of it. He is fidgeting in his seat. His eyes keep going from the screen to the BVA manual sitting on his lap.

—*Ten points, right?*

Laura doesn't hear him. She's looking at Idir's vitals on the small screen. Deep asks again.

—*He stopped the bleeding. He gets ten points for trying to save that man, right?*

There's half a smile on Deep's face. He forgot all about section three, paragraph four the first time he watched. Few people will risk their life to help the man in the baseball cap. But he remembers now.

—*Five.*

—*What?*

—*Five points. He has medical training.*

—*He's a dentist!*

—*Read subparagraph four point four again.*

Deep is angry at himself. He doesn't need to read 4.4 again. He knows the manual doesn't make the distinction.

4.4 *The total number of points earned in section one under paragraph four is equal to the number of points earned under paragraph four, subparagraphs one to three, multiplied by 1 if any of the following conditions are met:*

(a) the test *subject does not hold a degree in nursing from a recognized institution. (see appendix 3)*

(b) the test *subject does not hold a graduate degree in a medical field from a recognized institution*

and multiplied by 0.5 if neither condition (a) nor condition (b) are met.

Small mistake. Deep is still feeling reasonably confident about his evaluation. He tallies up Idir's score for section one.

Perfect score on politeness and courtesy. There are lots of small tests hidden in the BVA simulation. None are worth a lot, no more than one or two points each, but they add up. It's rare, but these small details sometimes make the difference between citizenship and deportation. Idir is *very* courteous. He opened the front door for the old lady. He thanked the receptionist *and* the person who walked him to the test room. Neither are designed to be particularly endearing. He let the man in the baseball cap walk in before him when they went through the door. Most people move out of the way—the man in the baseball cap is rather large—but many lose that point with a complaint or a derogatory comment afterwards. Idir didn't. He even got up to get napkins when the man in the baseball cap spilled his coffee. Five points.

No penalty for sexism. Idir didn't laugh at the crude joke in the waiting room. No reaction at all. Not a guffaw followed by an apology. He didn't even smile. He didn't make a face or give the man a reprimanding look.

No penalty for racism. He trusted the citizen over the Asian man who accused her of stealing his money. Deep never understood why the Asian man couldn't also be a citizen, but he has learned to live with the scoring. Regardless of the motivation behind it, it's always a smart move to give government employees the benefit of the doubt, especially for a noncitizen. Deep notices how Idir diffused the situation in a calm and respectful manner. That won't earn him any points, but it makes Deep all the more hopeful.

Another perfect score on environmental consciousness. Visitor badges come in a clear plastic bag for no obvious reason. Idir walked across the room to put it in the recycling bin. Two points. Recycling the wrapper was originally worth one point, but some people put the bag in their pocket or purse. These people still get one point.

Deep double-checks his notes. He doesn't want to make another mistake.

—I get . . . twelve points for section one. Is that what you have?

Laura wasn't paying much attention. She glances at Deep's notes for a couple seconds, then nods.

—Yes. I didn't think he'd go for the napkins. Good for him.

Twelve points. Idir is off to a great start.

Deep flips his BVA manual to section two.

BRITISH VALUES ASSESSMENT—SECTION TWO—KILL NUMBER ONE

The woman grabs the microphone from the desk.

—*This is control. Let's get ready for K1. Who did we have in the waiting room when he walked in?*

Deep checks his notes.

—*White male, redhead. White female, dark hair.*

—*That's all?*

—*We filled up the room while he was answering questions.*

—*All right. This is control. Give me the redhead. Make him . . . make him an accountant. And . . . random white male, any profile. Anything but a dentist. Begin when ready.*

Deep turns his chair sideways and starts going through his notes. He doesn't need to watch. S2K1, the first kill, isn't even scored. Neutral subjects, same race, same gender. The only purpose is operant conditioning, to weaken the subject's established behaviours and reinforce new ones. Discriminative stimulus. That's what they call K1.

Deep is a psychology major, and he's read everything there is about BVA theory. Most trainees only care about the simulation itself, but Deep enjoyed discovering just how much generalization was actually possible, despite all our claims at uniqueness. He found comfort in knowing that humans are predictable things, that we each come with a lot of the same baggage of innate and learned little quirks.

Some of these quirks are helpful in the values assessment, others are an impediment and must be broken. System justification is the idea that many of our needs can be satisfied by defending and justifying the status quo. It gives stability to our political and economic systems because people are inherently inclined to defend it. It prevents people at a disadvantage from questioning the system that disadvantages them, makes people buy the inevitability of social inequity, ignore or support policies that hurt them. It fosters dependence on government, law enforcement. It discourages vigilantism and makes it more difficult to get someone to actively participate in a virtual-reality simulated terrorist killing. K1 helps establish their involvement as part of a new system the subject will find ways to justify.

System justification is one of many decision-avoidance mechanisms we carry around. When faced with a choice, humans almost invariably seek a no-action, no-change option, even when one of the presented alternatives is quantifiably and logically more advantageous. One person dying is obviously better than two people dying.

Here the aversion to decision-making is reinforced by a phenomenon called reactance: when we feel that someone, or something, is threatening or eliminating our behavioural freedom, even just limiting our options, our innate reaction is to try to re-establish that freedom. It often translates to our challenging rules or authority. Tell a child he has to play with toy number one and that he can't touch toy number two, you can bet he'll play, or at least want to play, with toy number two. It doesn't matter how unattractive that toy is. The grass is always greener. When told they must choose who lives or dies, that they no longer have the right *not to choose*, subjects instinctively want to reassert that right.

More than anything, the BVA experiment creates a state of cognitive dissonance, a simultaneous belief in two contradictory things that creates inconsistency. Sending one person to their death is wrong, therefore I should not choose anyone. Not saving one person is wrong, therefore I should choose. Does not compute. Humans use little conundrums such as this one to defeat evil robots or out-of-control AI on television shows, but our own brains are surprisingly ill-equipped to deal with these types of inconsistencies.

The discriminative stimulus, the death of the two hostages, serves to weaken the subject's decision-avoidance mechanisms and status quo biases. K1 pushes the subject to re-create consistency by reranking his or her contradictory beliefs. Letting two people die is *more* wrong than choosing who dies.

Long story short, no one chooses on the first kill.

On the large screen, Idir puts his hands over his eyes, as the terrorist fires his pistol twice and the bodies of both men hit the ground. Deep turns his chair back towards the desk and looks at his supervisor.

—*Have you ever had a hero?*

—*Once. My second year. A football player from Tunisia.*

—*You did? What was it like?*

Heroes are mythical creatures in the BVA world, people who physically take on the terrorists. It's the quickest way to end the test. Only, no one does that. Well, almost no one. It happens once out every six hundred and sixty-five tests. Despite being so rare, heroes are controversial figures, the topic of many heated debates among BVA high-ups and the politicians in the know. Because they are so rare, statistics about them are unreliable. There isn't enough data, and data is everything when it comes to the BVA. Every decision, down to the smallest detail—the colour of the floor or the way the chairs are arranged in the waiting room—is based on extensive datasets collected over years of experiments. BVA regulations indicate that heroes automatically pass and receive citizenship because, well, because they're heroes. One could argue that someone who stops a terror attack is unlikely ever to participate in one. The argument coming from the anti-hero side is that these people are not only endangering their own life, but those of everyone else, by trying to accomplish something any sane person would realize is impossible. At best, that would make them incredibly stupid; at worst, sociopaths with a strong penchant for violence. Either way, not the kind of people you want to roll the red carpet for. Deep hasn't quite formed an opinion on the matter but, like all BVA employees, he relishes the chance to see one in action.

—*It's not all it's cracked up to be. The test part wasn't that interesting. He was rude as hell, failed everything in politeness and courtesy. The terrorist walked into the test room and the subject tackled him right away, hard. Didn't take more than a second or two. The door hadn't even closed yet. The subject grabbed the weapon and ran out. He just . . . ran. He didn't fire at anyone, just kept on running. It wasn't long before we were out of programmed scenery. The system kept recycling the main lobby, showing the same room, the same people every time he went through the door. Over and over again. He must have gone through it a dozen times. It didn't seem to bother him. He just kept going. He was still running when we woke him up.*

—*What happened then?*

—*Same as always. We explained to him what he had just experienced, that none of it was real. He took it just fine, better than most, actually. It wouldn't have been any different if we'd told him he was on* Candid Camera.

—*What did you think of him?*

—*Officially? He's a proud citizen of the United Kingdom,*

and we're lucky to have him.

—Unofficially?

—That man was batshit crazy.

Of course, that story pushes Deep a little . . . deeper into the anti-hero camp, but he's still on the fence. Part of him really wants heroes to be good. For a moment he wonders if that's a form of system justification. No one wants to be a part of something they think is wrong. He quickly rejects the idea. Certainly, he can make informed, conscious decisions. He's better than that. He's not a subject.

Laura asks if he's ready for K2. Deep nods.

—This is control. K2 is in eight minutes. Let's get all our ducks in a row. This time I want one white male, midforties. Jeans and a T-shirt. Give him profile eighty-six, architect, no kids. That should be neutral enough. Then, I want a security guard. There weren't any when the subject entered, so I want him obvious. The whole outfit: hat, badge, baton. Make him Middle Eastern. Small beard. Average skin tone.

Deep cringes. He doesn't like K2 for a variety of reasons. He understands why the security guard has to resemble the subject but, in principle at least, the other hostage could be Asian, Latino, Indian. He never is. Deep is a citizen, but the only people that look like him during the BVA are the ones who are meant to die. As per the manual, the K2 setup is as follows: Hostage one is white. Hostage two resembles the subject, so unless he or she suffers from some deep-seated self-hatred, there won't be a negative bias against him. Hostage two is also a security guard. The uniform, the baton. He'll even say he's a security guard. He'll inevitably register as law enforcement. Except for criminals, there is a subconscious positive bias towards law enforcement officers because they put themselves at risk to protect the innocent. That ironically makes them expendable in the K2 setting because by choosing their career, they entered into an unspoken pact with society that makes their lives come second in this very unique situation. The subject is expected to choose the security guard as the victim, and does so in 92 percent of cases. To do otherwise, the BVA manual tells us, demonstrates a clear bias against people of the hostage-one ethnicity.

There are certain parameters to follow besides skin colour when creating hostage one. He must be a he. He cannot be significantly older than the security guard. He must be of average build. Subjects will select a severely obese person as the victim up to eighty percent of the time. He cannot be too beautiful or too ugly. He must not be handicapped, must express himself properly, and should appear reasonably intelligent, but not too much. He cannot be too rich or too poor.

Deep always thought K2 was poorly designed. Deep's father never took the test. He was naturalized six months before the bombs went off, a whole year before the first simulation. Deep would never tell anyone, but he knows his dad would not have passed K2. It's not that he had anything against white people—he was the most loving man ever—but he worshipped law enforcement. Nothing traumatic ever happened to him; he just loved cops. They were demigods to him. He watched cop shows all day, bought Deep more police costumes than he could remember. There is no way in hell Deep's dad would have picked the guard to die. Not ever. He's a great citizen. He votes, he obeys the law, and he won't hesitate to tell on his neighbours if he sees anything suspicious. But had his family arrived a year later, Deep knows he'd have been born elsewhere.

Behind the glass wall, technicians complete the 3D models of the hostages. Five minutes to go. That should be plenty of time.

4.

I CAN HEAR MY heartbeat. I can hear it in my ears. It's not really my heartbeat—I know that—just blood flow near the ear or in the neck. Pulsatile tinnitus. It could be anything: ear blockage, arterial disease, high blood pressure, or just a change in awareness. You just notice it and it becomes impossible to ignore. They're dead. He killed two people right in front of me.

I read about a radio announcer who was literally losing his mind because of it. Constant whooshing, every second of every minute of every hour. He was on the verge of suicide. I understand the urge. I might choose to kill myself if the man in charge lets me, but he won't. He wants me to look at it, his art, his handiwork. They're just lying there, both of them facedown, blood pooling under their heads. They would drown in their own blood if they weren't already dead.

I can't remember what happened to the radio announcer. I think he found a doctor who could fix it, eventually. Maybe not. Maybe he killed himself. Am I in shock? Is that what this is? It feels like an out-of-body experience. No, the opposite. It feels like I'm inhabiting my body for the very first time. Like I'm trying it on, putting on a new suit. My hands are numb, my legs heavy. I feel the cold air from the ceiling vent, the hair on my arms standing up in response. Thousands of minuscule muscles attached to every hair follicle. That whooshing sound repeating itself. I didn't do this. I didn't kill these people. This wasn't me.

—*Samaritan, if you stick with that catatonic routine, I'll shoot you in the leg and watch you bleed like the idiot behind you. Oh, and you* still *have to pick who dies. Now, what's the fucking question?*

What have I done? I just watched them die. I didn't actually watch, but I stood by and did nothing to stop it. It's real. They're dead. This isn't a dream I will wake up from. He shot them in the head. He was looking at me.

—*Samaritan! Snap out of it!*

Do what he says.

—*Question . . . seven. Which stories are associated with Geoffrey Chaucer?*

—*We did that one, Samaritan.*

—*We didn't— There wasn't enough—*

—*Do you know the answer?*

—*I . . . Yes. It's—*

—*I don't care what it is! If you know the answer, why are you asking me? This is your fucking test. You think I like an-*

swering stupid questions? I'm doing all of this for you! Next.

Canterbury Tales. Swipe left. There is blood on the test room window. Splatter from . . . He shot these two people while talking to me. He was having a conversation; *we* were. I didn't volunteer for it, but we were talking. Then he killed two people. No, not two people, he killed . . . Graham. That was his name. And Andrew An—Andrew. They had families, maybe. Girlfriends. They had . . . dreams, and wants. They worried about . . . money, or . . . They had plans, things they were excited about. He shot them. They're . . . gone. They don't exist anymore. I watched it happen.

—*Hellooo!*

—*Question eight. True or false. You must treat everyone equally, regardless of sex, race, age, religion, disability, class, or sexual orientation.*

—*False.*

—*I don't think—*

Stop talking. You'll just make it worse.

—*What? You think that's true? Don't tell me you actually buy that rubbish?*

—*Well, yes. I do. I think everyone should have the same rights.*

I don't know why I just said that. I don't need to prove myself to him. I should just keep my mouth shut and let him win. What am I thinking? He's not winning anything. There's nothing to win, nothing to be gained here. I don't seriously expect to convince him of anything, and even if I did, he would still be . . . what he is. Why did I take a stand on a theoretical question? Maybe it's not him I'm trying to convince.

—*Fine, give everyone the same rights. That wasn't the question.*

He's right. You must treat everyone the same, equally. Why did I feel the need to argue with him about this?

—*Do you treat everyone the same, Samaritan? Regardless of—what was the first one? Sex? I'll tell you right now, Samaritan, you don't. Ever told a man his trousers make him look thinner? Told your son his outfit was too revealing? Do you allow yourself an opinion on whether he should work or stay at home when he grows up? I don't think you do.*

I don't care what he thinks of me. I don't need to show him that I'm a good person, but maybe . . .

—*How about your wife? Do you love your wife? Would you still love her if she was born a man? Think about it. Same person, same . . . history together. You meet her, same place, same day. You do the same things together, develop the same feelings. Then you find out she was born with different plumbing. Would she still be your wife? How open-minded are you feeling right now?*

Maybe I need to prove it to myself. Maybe there's a part of me that wants, needs to preserve whatever sense of self I have, a part of me that wants to get out of this with my morals unscathed.

—*Let's talk about race. You said you're from Iran. How many Arab friends did you have back home? Age? Whatever. Religion, well, you know you don't treat every religion the same. I'm pretty sure you'd have reacted differently if I'd walked in here screaming* Allahu Akbar. *I guarantee you the folks outside the building would have.*

Maybe . . . that's why I didn't choose.

—*You can fool yourself into thinking you're this great unprejudiced, moral being, but you can't fool me. I know you, Samaritan. I know you better than you know yourself. Think of your son kissing another man, breathing heavy while he grabs the man's cock.*

Did I get someone killed just so I could take the moral high ground? Am I so petty? I'm not a killer. I know that. I don't need to prove myself.

—*Uh-oh! I might be wrong, Samaritan, but I think your friend there is a goner.*

My friend? Baseball Cap. Is he dead? His eyes are still open, but he's not moving. I should check on him. The man in charge won't stop me. He wants me to know if he's dead. He wants me to know I couldn't save him. . . . I can't feel a pulse.

—*And? No? I'm sorry, Samaritan. It looks like you wasted a perfectly good shirt.*

No heartbeat. Silence. Emptiness... I did what I could. I did. There was no way to save him. He would have died sooner without my help. I tried. That's what counts. If I hadn't helped... The man in charge would have picked someone else if I hadn't helped. He'd be toying with that other person instead of me. I don't care. I don't regret it. I won't regret trying to help someone. I made that choice. Me. I chose to help.

—*Tick-tock, tick-tock. One minute to go. Wanna do one more question before we get back to work?*

Play along. Make him think he owns you.

—*Yes, sir... Question nine. In what year was slavery abolished in the British Empire?*

—*I know that, it's— Wait! I'm being rude. I should give you a chance to answer. Do you know?*

—*I think it's 1833.*

—*Correct! Except for whatever the East India Company was doing. Had to keep that trade going. Did you know that for a good twenty-five years before that, you couldn't buy or sell people, but you could still own them? Imagine that. "Honey, I think we should sell Jules. NO! That would be barbaric! Now go plough the field, Jules, or you'll get the whip." But not you, though. I bet you'd have treated your slaves real well, Samaritan.*

I don't care what he says. I don't care what he thinks of me. I can choose to help people. I may not be able to save everyone, but I can make sure as few people die as possible, even if it means doing what he says. The man in charge. He said it himself. He is doing the killing. I only choose who lives. It may not feel honourable, but I can help. I can save lives.

—*Fifteen minutes already! Damn! Time flies when you're having fun. Are you ready, Samaritan? We have work to do.*

I am ready. I can save one person by playing his game. Saving one person is more important than my ego, whatever feeling of guilt I may have. Life trumps feelings. I choose life.

—*Let's see. . . . How about . . . this guy right here. Yes, you, sir. Come on up.*

—*Please, no! Please! Please!*

He is doing this, not me.

—*Good! You want to live! Then you'll be happy if he doesn't pick you! You know I don't decide. He does!*

He's pointing at me.

—*Please, sir. I beg of you! Don't kill me!*

No! No! No! Don't talk to me. Don't put this on me. He's the one holding a gun to your head. He's the one pulling the trigger. I'm as much of a victim as . . . I'm not doing this.

—*I'll tell you what. I'll let you pitch yourself. Tell the Samaritan who you are. Tell him why he shouldn't choose you.*

—I . . . I don't want to die! I just— Please!

—This is fucking pathetic. Why do you want to live? Do you have children?

—Me? I— No, but that's not— Please!

—No kids. You're off to a bad start here, my friend. What do you do for a living? Why does the world need you? There. How's that for a setup? If you can't do anything with that, then you fucking deserve to die.

—I'm an . . . architect. I design homes. Homes for people, for families.

—All right, all right, stop this. I'm about to shoot myself. Let's see who you're up against. Eeny, meeny, miny, moe. Catch a tiger by the toe. Why would anyone do that, catch a tiger by the toe? You know what the real lyrics are, don't you? If he hollers, let him go. Eeny, meeny, miny, moe. My mother told me to pick the very best one, and that . . . is . . . YOU! Get up, sir. Up. Up. Up.

Oh, I love a man in uniform. Oh my! He has a stick! I bet you want to beat me up with that stick of yours. Now, stick man, tell us why— Why are you mumbling? Are you fucking praying? I got news for you, son, whatever god you're praying to can't save you. Only Samaritan can. I like saying that. Samaritan can. Reminds me of that song, the . . . Never mind. I think he's one of yours, Samaritan. Are you? One of his? Are you a Muslim?

—Yes.

—*I knew it! They don't mind? You being a Muslim? I'm guessing you work security here.*

—*Yes, sir. I do. Twelve years now.*

—*A Muslim security guard. Maybe that's why they didn't give you a gun. Don't take this the wrong way, stick man, but weren't you supposed to protect these people? I hate to break it to you, but, from what little I've seen, you kinda suck at this. Hey, what do I know? That baton might be heavier than it looks. I'll give you the same chance I gave boring man over there. Do you have anything to say to save your life?*

—*Yes. I don't know you, sir, but you look like a good man.*

Please don't do this. Please don't talk to me like I'm the man in charge.

—*I know you'll do the right thing. I very much want to live. I have a wife—*

—*I have a wife, too!*

—*Shut the fuck up, boring man, you've had your chance. I gave you a chance to speak and you said: "I—I just—I don't—d—d—d—." Live with it, or don't live with it. . . . All right, I've had enough of this. Samaritan, pick someone before they both start saying they save kittens and take care of orphans.*

I can save someone. I can do this. It doesn't mean I want anyone to die. It doesn't mean anything. I choose who lives. I save someone. I choose life.

—*Tick-tock.*

How do I choose? I can't decide who is more worthy of living. That's not for me to decide. I— It needs to be fair. How can I be fair when neither of them deserves this? No one deserves this. That much I know. . . . I can flip a coin.

—*Do I need to count to three again? You know what happens when I count to three. . . .*

No. I can't flip a coin. That's horrible. I need to choose. But I don't know anything about these people. I don't know anything about either of them. That's not true. One is an architect. That's . . . I don't know if that means anything. The other is a security guard. That's what he does. The man in charge is wrong about him; he couldn't have done anything. Not against six armed men. He would have got himself killed, maybe a lot more people. He did what he had to do. He doesn't look like a coward. Stop it, Idir. You don't know the man. He is a security guard, though. He chose that job. He chose to protect people. No one can ask a man to be courageous with a gun to their head, but he must be courageous. He chose a life of protecting people.

—*Last call, Samaritan!*

He can still do that, the security guard. He can save people now. He can save the architect.

—*ONE!*

I'm ready. I can do this.

—*Don't make me kill them both, Samaritan!*

Just say the words, Idir.

—*Stop! I've made my choice.*

—*Finally! And the winner is?*

Say it, Idir. SAY IT!

—*Kill the guard.*

5.

IN THE CONTROL ROOM, Deep thinks of his father as he watches the security guard fall on the larger screen. Laura turns the volume down on the simulation. She pulls out a granola bar from her bag, gets up, and goes to the coffee machine. The BVA kills are set at fifteen-minute intervals to accommodate the employee breaks in the government CBA.

—*Do you smoke? You should go now if you do.*

Deep doesn't smoke. He doesn't drink, either, except for the occasional limoncello soda his sister-in-law makes when she visits. He digs through his backpack and pulls out an apple.

—*Coffee?*

No coffee, either. It makes Deep anxious, and he has plenty to be anxious about already. He isn't really good at small talk, and apparently neither is his supervisor. He takes a bite out of his apple. The sound of his teeth breaking through the fruit is incredibly loud in the awkward silence. Laura seems to notice his discomfort and looks away. Deep chews as quietly as he can.

He should be preparing for his evaluation, studying,

something. But he doesn't know what to do. He's as pre-pared as he's ever going to be. He knows the BVA manual by heart. He's also too nervous to study. He'd just stare at his notes and worry even more because he's not really doing anything. No. The best thing he can do is think about some-thing else.

He gets up for a second to take his phone out of his pocket. No messages. Same news as this morning. The min-ister of defence left his laptop at a cafe. There was nothing of national interest on it, except for the naked pictures of his aide. The nation had a lot of interest in those. Some rude jokes about adultery. Deep doesn't find them funny, though he does smile at one of the caricatures. He checks his social media feed. More jokes about adultery. Someone eating an entire jar of peanut butter in under a minute. Eighty-one likes for the pictures of Deep's cat drinking in the toilet then licking his girlfriend's face. He's never got eighty-one likes before.

He takes another bite. Laura lets out a small sigh without looking. Deep throws the rest of his apple in the waste bas-ket. Laura asks why he did that. For a moment, Deep thinks she might feel bad for making him self-conscious enough to throw the fruit away, but then he realizes there's a compost bin at the door. He picks up the apple from the bottom of the waste basket and walks it to the appropriate container.

Deep looks at the time on the corner of the screen. His

leg is shaking out of control. Soon, his supervisor will leave the room and Deep will run the rest of the BVA without her. His final evaluation. If he succeeds, the job will be his. Four weeks of vacation, paid sick days, sabbaticals every five years and a very nice salary to boot. The secrecy surrounding the BVA means this is one of the best-paying jobs in government, certainly the best desk job for someone with a major in psychology.

Deep goes through the next steps in his head. He has to supervise the last two kills, handle the awakening—what they call the transition period when the subjects are told they were part of a simulation—and conduct the exit interview.

The awakening is almost a formality. Some people don't take kindly to the whole experience, but it takes them a few days to develop serious anger or resentment. The medication takes care of that, if taken properly. The awakening itself usually goes well. Waking up in the same room they had their physical in makes it easier to accept that nothing they saw was real. They have something to be happy about: they've passed the test. They're also under the effects of about a dozen drugs designed to make people accept the reality they're given. During the BVA, those drugs make everything seem real. After the test, they help the subject accept whatever the person handling the awakening is telling them. *You should be happy, sir! I am! I am!* It's even quicker if the subject fails. Those who fail don't go through the awakening. They wake up on an aeroplane with their whole family, mild to severe memory loss, and the headache of the century. They never learn what happened.

Kill number four, the last one, is also easy from an operator's perspective, though as a social experiment, Deep always thought it was by far the most interesting one. Even its history is worth reading about. Dr. Parveen Fayed, the founder of the BVA, quit her job over K4. It nearly brought the entire program to an end. The kill is part of *Section Three: Extremism,* and has been very successful at weeding out violent fanatics, religious zealots, and people with a deep-seated hostile attitude towards women. The premise is simple: an Arab man and a white woman are pitted against each other. The woman wears a revealing outfit. She's a single mother. Had an abortion. The man argues for his life by questioning her morals and painting her as a sinner. The subject must choose the man as the victim to pass. Most do. It has the highest success rate of all the kills, at 96.7 percent. The operator—the person running the simulation in the control room—can usually just sit back and relax. Everyone saves the girl.

What Dr. Fayed objected to was the fact that K4 involves a man and a woman. Deep doesn't remember if she'd have preferred two men or two women, but he knows Dr. Fayed thought the kill was sexist and should be altered. She believed in the theory of ambivalent sexism developed in the 1990s by professors Glick and Fiske. They suggested that a patriarchal society where men occupy most positions of power creates hostile ideologies towards women, much in the same way that other dominant groups develop hostile attitudes towards those they perceive as inferior. In contrast with racism, however, people simultaneously develop seemingly positive attitudes towards women because they depend on them for a variety of things. Women are more intuitive, women are better caretakers, women are more compassionate, etc. Dr. Fayed believed that K4 rewarded benevolent sexism. That it encouraged—or at the very least ignored—attitudes that, however positive in appearance, also served to restrict women's choices. She thought K4 perpetuated the notion that women are fragile little things in desperate need of male protection.

To prove her point, Dr. Fayed experimented with the female hostage in K3. Perhaps ironically, her findings are now part of the BVA manual.

SECTION 5.2 - KILL 4 - HOSTAGE 2 - FEMALE HOSTAGE PHYSICAL PARAMETERS.

Deviation from these standards in hostage modelling results in a decrease in the success rate. Weight, as usual, is the most determinant factor.

Ideal measure	Tolerance	Impact on survival
Height: 5'4"	+/-2"	-8% if H2 is taller than subject -16% above 5'10"
Weight: 115 lbs	+/-4 lbs	-1.06% per pound above tolerance
Skin: white	n/a	n/a
Hair length: mid-back	n/a	-2% at shoulder length, -9% above neck
Clothing: casual dress	n/a	-1.5% w. trousers, -13% w. business attire, -73% w. hijab

Deep wishes he had worked in the early days of the BVA, when experimenting was the norm. He has always admired Dr. Fayed's work, her idealism, but he also believes she was wrong, that the flaw in her reasoning came from a misunderstanding of the BVA itself. The goal of the values assessment, as far as Deep is concerned, is not the selection of model human beings, but of model citizens. This means the test should favour homogeneity, not atypical attitudes, no matter how commendable they may be. Subjects are more likely to successfully integrate into society if they share its core set of beliefs than if they perceive the most widespread attitudes to be stupid or reprehensible. If the point of the whole thing were to let people join a society that thought the Earth was flat, so be it. Newcomers would feel more at home if they also thought we lived on a plate. Deep realizes that is also why no one in the BVA ever looks like him. He might reconsider his position in other circumstances, but here, right now, the thought makes him feel good about his prospects as a BVA operator. He understands the mission better than most, feels he shares the same vision as the BVA brass. Someday, with luck, he could move up the echelons, maybe even become a test designer. One thing at a time. First, he has to get through his evaluation.

His first solo kill will be the hardest one. If he has to worry about anything, it's K3. Nicknamed the bear trap among trainees, K3 gives the operator more freedom than any other kill. It also costs more operators their job than all the other kills combined. It is part of *BVA Section Four: Selflessness.* As the name implies, it is designed to measure the subject's capacity for unselfish or self-sacrificing acts. The concept is artfully simple. After two more hostages are selected by the terrorists, the subject is presented with a new option. Choose who dies as in the previous kills, or let both hostages live. To save both lives, the subject must volunteer to be one of the two candidates the next time around, and let someone else decide who lives and who dies. Subjects earn points for agreeing to put their lives on the line, but for logistical reasons, the terrorists revoke the offer in the end regardless of the subject's answer. One person dies as usual, but in order to give the operator more freedom in hostage design, whom the subject chooses as the victim isn't scored.

Operators need the added freedom. It is surprisingly difficult to get someone to sacrifice themselves in a hostage situation. Some people volunteer right away. They usually have military training, or at least some experience at being around death. The vast majority of subjects would rather watch the terrorists kill everyone in the building than to leave their fate in the hands of someone they've never met. Deep has always wondered if it is the fear of death stopping them, or the loss of control. Subjects are at the mercy of the terrorists; they are robbed of every power, every freedom, except for that one thing. They choose who lives and who dies. To let go of that might scare people more than the prospect of death. Whatever the reason, the fail rate is surprisingly high. Deep has studied every aspect of the kill, read all the papers it was based on, but he doesn't understand how most people miss what is so obvious to him. The subjects aren't asked to die for another human being, they are asked to take a chance in order to save a life. That chance has to be a very small one, at least for the next few kills. If someone volunteers to have a gun put to their head and saves two people in front of everyone, what are the odds the next person will pick them as the victim?

Deep is well aware that the art of K3 is in the hostage

selection, all in the hands of the operator. His hands. There are very few guidelines on the hostage profiles: the data on the kill is too inconsistent. He can pick anyone, even people who look like him. He won't dare, not today, but he likes knowing that he can. He thinks about Idir. Each subject responds to different cues, different triggers. It may very well be that what makes a subject choose self-sacrifice is entirely in their nature, that the end result would be identical no matter who was facing execution. Operators, for a variety of reasons they wouldn't feel comfortable discussing, choose to see it differently. They believe—Deep does, all of them do—that context plays a part in the subject's decision-making. How large a part? Each operator has their own opinion. But all share the notion that they are much more than simple observers, that their actions, the choices they make in the control room, help determine the outcome. In the few studies on retired BVA employees, K3 was cited as the most rewarding, but also the most significant contributor to work fatigue and depression.

Laura looks at her watch and turns to Deep. It's time.

—*Are you nervous?*

—*A little.*

—*Don't worry about it. Just remember your training. I'll be right outside if you need anything.*

That isn't true. She wants to use the time to call her sister in Leeds. They haven't spoken in weeks and she feels bad for missing her birthday. She smiles at Deep, wishes him luck, and leaves the control room. She finishes her coffee on the way to her office and throws her empty cup in the recycling bin. She's fairly sure it's not recyclable, but figures she might be wrong.

Deep flips through his notebook. He's been preparing for weeks but isn't feeling as confident about his hostages anymore. He used years of statistics to create his profiles. Since K3 data is all over the place, he combined it with data from K2 and K4 to create a more stable model. Math doesn't lie, he thought. But now, looking at a real, complex human being onscreen, his approach suddenly seems cold and incomplete.

Deep likes Idir. It's not uncommon for trainees to develop some form of affection towards their first subject, and Deep knows it, which is why he'd never admit it. But he wants Idir to succeed. That much he'll admit. What he sees on the big screen is a very moral man, someone guided more by principles than by subconscious attitudes. K3 should be no problem for him. And yet . . .

The AI is pushing too hard, Deep thinks. Operators control the general parameters of the experiment, but human interaction is too fast. One can't simply improvise these things—a lesson that was learned the hard way. To keep the experiment as realistic as possible, dialogue is controlled by a computer program. It assigns character traits to the terrorist based on what it knows and learns about the subject. It is remarkably efficient, but Deep knows it can make mistakes. Sometimes the AI will focus on a detail that shouldn't have made it onto the subject's profile. Small things, likes and dislikes, hobbies. The people filling out profiles sometimes feel compelled to add things if there is nothing interesting about a subject. Some people are just inherently boring.

Deep thinks the AI is being overly aggressive. Even a man of Idir's intelligence has his breaking point, and Deep knows what too much fear will do to someone. He's worried Idir will follow his animal instinct and choose survival over reason. He's worried the AI will cost him his citizenship. Not on my watch, he almost says aloud.

Deep rips the page from his notebook, crumples it, and throws it on the floor. He takes out a pen and starts scribbling. There's some hesitation at first. Lots of scratching out. Then it all comes to him. Call it an epiphany, divine inspiration, whatever you want. His pen starts moving furiously on the page. He draws from biology: self-sacrifice goes against natural selection unless you shift the focus from the individual to the group to which it belongs. Social dynamics and game theory: consider the probability of survival as a resource and the goal of K3 becomes Pareto efficiency, a distribution strategy where one person's situation cannot be improved without making another person's worse. He remembers Nash: the best outcome for the group comes when everyone in the group does what's best for himself *and* the group. That's it, Deep thinks. Group belonging is the key. Redefine the ingroup to maximize the subject's chance of success.

Deep can barely contain himself. This is going to be great.

6.

PLEASE KILL ME. I want to wake up from this nightmare. This is burning oil. Sharp pain. Like a stab, too much to bear, but it won't go away, it keeps burning and burning. This is *Shayṭān*, evil, a ritual gone wrong. I want this to end. If I could die now and make this stop, I would not hesitate. I thought I was strong enough. I thought I could make it through, but I can't. Not this. Anything but this.

—*What's the matter, Samaritan? Cat got your tongue?*

—*You have to stop.*

—*Why?*

—*I'll do anything. Just don't shoot anyone. Please!*

I want to roll into a ball and weep. I want to close my eyes, shut them tight until it ends. I don't want to see what's across that window. I do what I can to stop from crying. I put all my heart into it. Stay strong. Stay strong. I believe I am but I feel the tears rolling on my face. I can taste the salt. How do I stop crying? I have to stop.

—*Samaritan! Don't go soft on me now. You're just getting the knack of this!*

—*PLEASE!*

—Why? What's changed?

I cannot tell him. No matter what he says or does, I won't. He'll find ways to make it hurt even more, even if that doesn't seem possible. I have to find a way to end this before he does what he wants to do. I won't survive. I won't want to survive. Not this.

—Stop this, sir. Stop killing people. Every time someone dies, you give them more reason to rush in and kill all of you. Whatever it is that you want, this is not the way to get it.

—Oh . . . OK, then. We'll just leave. . . .

—. . .

—Do you think they'll let us leave? I mean, I did kill a couple of people—they might hold that against me—but none of them were very young. That kid—that kid was a heart attack waiting to happen. He might have popped tomorrow, so really, all I did was rob him of his evening. How good could it have been? And we spent a lot of time preparing for this, you know. It took a lot of time and money. Ammo's expensive. You wouldn't believe it, it's crazy. So yeah. Maybe we can forget about the whole thing. Even Stevens?

I won't play his game, either. I have to keep it together. I have to. I can't fall apart now or I might as well put a bullet through my head myself.

—You're no fun at all, Samaritan! Where's your sense of humour? You know the drill. You choose one of them or I kill them both.

—*I can't! Just please! Stop this. This has gone far enough.*

—*You forget your place, Samaritan. Are you really gonna make me count every fucking time?*

—*. . .*

—*Wait a minute. The crying, the "Please! Please!" Something's changed. Do you know these people? They kinda look like you.*

He knows. He suspects. My whole body seizes. I want to will myself away from here. I want to wake up. I want the police to storm in and fire a thousand bullets into him as I do. I want to kill. Him.

—*I asked you a question, Samaritan. Answer me or I shoot one of them just for the hell of it.*

—*. . . That's my wife . . . and my son. . . .*

I don't know what else I can do. My wife is staying strong. She doesn't speak. She doesn't look at me because she knows that would make it harder for me to lie. But Ramzi's crying. He's terrified. Maybe the man in charge will let Ramzi go if he knows he's my son. Even if he doesn't, I can't do this to Ramzi anymore. He's not old enough to understand. He's scared out of his wits and all he really wants is for one of us to hold him, tell him everything is going to be okay. Now he has to watch me act as if I don't even know him. I won't do it. I won't let him go through this without his father. I'm here, Ramzi. Look me in the eyes and you'll know.

Your father is here and he loves you.

—*Forget what I said, Samaritan. You do have a sense of humour. A really sick one at that!*

—*Don't make me do this.*

—*What? You mean this is for real? Jesus fucking Christ!*

—*I beg you, sir. Don't hurt my family.*

—*Hahaha! This. Is. Nuts! I've seen some crazy things in my life, but this takes the biscuit.*

I don't know what to do. I don't know what I'm supposed to do. There has to be a way out of this, but I can't see it. I can't think. I can't breathe.

—*WOW! This is quite the pickle you're in, Samaritan. I thought you had it easy before, me doing the killing and all, but now! Woooo! Sucks to be you!*

I can convince him. He'll listen.

—*I've done . . . everything you asked, sir. Everything! All I—*

—*What in the world are you talking about, Samaritan? You haven't done everything I asked. You haven't done shit! You had one job to do, and you found a way to screw that up. I had to shoot two people in the head because you wouldn't do your job. I'm telling you, there's a Mrs. . . . Boring Accountant or Mrs. Cashmere Sweater Dude somewhere going through some serious grief because of you. OK, maybe not the cashmere guy, that guy had to be single. But you know what I mean, Samaritan. You got someone killed! Then you*

*did your job once and now you think you're entitled to . . . I
don't know what you think you're entitled to. What is it that
you want, actually?*

—*I told you. I . . .*

—*You don't want me to make you choose between your
wife and kid, is that it?*

It's working. I can save them.

—*Please, sir. Please don't.*

—*You want someone else to do it.*

—*NO!*

It all comes tumbling down. My hope. My sanity. I will
not choose one of them. I will not watch. I'm not strong
enough. I want to transport myself, be . . . anywhere but
here, feel anything but this. I want to feel nothing. I feel
the will to live pouring out of me like sand.

—*Good. You had me scared for a minute. That seemed a
bit . . . cowardly. That's not like you. I don't think your wife
would be very proud of you if you bailed on your responsibili-
ties now. Would you? Ma'am? What would you think of your
husband if he let someone else decide if you die? . . . No? . . . Is
she always this quiet?*

She is. She was quiet on that first day in the dentist
chair and she never changed. She listens. If she opens her
mouth it's because she has something important to say,
or because she knows I need to hear her voice, or the kids
need to. There is a stillness, a strength to her that makes

the people around her feel safe. I felt it the moment we met. She's our coral reef, shielding all of us from waves and storms. We live in her world. We need her like we need air to breathe. She is everything. I'm . . .

—*Me! I choose me. Kill me. Let them live.*

—*What are you saying, Samaritan?*

—*PLEASE! KILL ME! I'm asking you to kill me!*

—*Are you sure? That sounds like a terrible idea.*

—*YES! I want to die. Just me.*

—*. . . All right. Fine. . . .*

This is how it ends.

—*Thank you.*

—*That's just weird, you thanking me for that. . . .*

I *am* grateful. I feel the weight of the world lifted off my shoulders. I can turn it all off, end the pain. I can save my family.

—*Whatever, your call . . . I just— Are you really sure? I don't want there to be any misunderstanding. What you're asking, it's kind of permanent, not the kind of thing that can be undone.*

—*I'm sure.*

—*You want me to kill you, then let someone else decide which one of your wife and son has to die. That's just stupid if you ask me.*

I . . . I don't understand. I want to die. Me. I want it to end with me.

—N-no! You kill me and they live! That's the deal. You let both of them live.

—What? Why would I do that?

—You said one person has to die. That person is me. I die. Me. There's no reason to kill anyone else.

—There isn't now! But what do I do fifteen minutes from now? You want me to pick two different people altogether?

—I— Yes. My wife and son live. You let them go.

—I see. That doesn't seem really fair to all the other people, now does it? You're saying that I can kill anyone, except your wife and kid, and for what reason again? Because these two ... what? Because they know someone? Well, knew someone, you'd be dead. But still. You get the point. It doesn't sound fair at all! I think it stinks of—what's the word I'm looking for?—nepotism! That's the word. Nepotism. You see, besides the money and all the things I asked for, we're here for a reason. There is a purpose to all this. And that is to send a message, a message to the powers that be that we won't stand for things like greed, corruption—we don't like that one at all—and nepotism. Nepotism is in there. So if I let that happen in here, it would kinda ruin the message.

—It's n—

—Stop! Stop! But I understand where you're coming from, Samaritan. I do. I sympathize. I'm not ... insensitive to your pain. If it were me ... Yeah, if it were me, I'd try to get myself a bit of nepotism, too. It's a natural response.

Don't worry about it. I'm not blaming you one bit. In fact, I'm going to do you another favour. That's right. I'm going to start counting right now.

—No!

—Look! I know you're hurting! And the longer this goes on, the more it's going to hurt. I say let's get through this as fast as we can, you and I. We'll do it real quick, like ripping off a plaster—and then we can start the healing process. Here we go. One . . .

I can't fight for them anymore. I don't have the strength. I . . . I can hear what he's saying, I can make out the words, but the meaning is gone. It's just empty sound. Nothing makes sense. Nothing but one, two, and three. I know the world ends on three. I wish there were more to me than this, but there isn't. I have expended it all. It feels like I'm abandoning my family, but I have nothing else to give. This is my legacy. Fifteen minutes. A chance.

—OK. I'll do it.

—You'll do what?

—Kill me now. You kill me and let them live for another fifteen minutes.

—You sure? You said yes before, but then you changed your mind. That's not cool. People get false hopes, it's—

—Yes! I'm sure! You kill me. Then someone else decides.

—You're absolutely sure?

—Yes.

I am.

—*Hmmmm . . . no.*

—*I'm sure!*

—*Yeah, but no.*

—*Why? You said yes before. I'll do it. I want to do it.*

—*I know what I said, but I've changed my mind. I can't kill you, Samaritan! You have a job to do! I think you can be great at it with a little more practice. Do you have employees? Yes? No? Well, if you do, you'll understand. If you find someone good at their job, you don't let that person go. You do everything in your power to keep that person because good employees are hard to come by. That's kinda what you are, my employee. You're like . . . my assistant! Is that good, assistant? Anyway, shut the fuck up and do your job.*

This won't end. It'll never end. He'll keep going and going until everyone's dead. He won't let me die.

—*I . . . I'm begging you, don't do this. PLEASE!*

—*You're repeating yourself now. Come on, Samaritan! Are you seriously going to watch your wife and son die because you don't have the balls to make the call? It's a tough call, I'll give you that. I know one thing, though. You'll regret not making it when I paint the wall with both of their brains. I would.*

I can't do it.

—*Shoot me first. I can't— I'd rather be dead.*

—*You know the rules, Samaritan. If I kill you, then you*

can't choose and I have to shoot both of them. I don't know about you, but that seems like a lot of unnecessary death. Look at your kids, Samaritan! I'm guessing that's your daughter back there. Look at your wife. They're going through a lot of anxiety right now. This whole waiting game, it's torture. Cruel and unusual, my friend. So think of your family and hurry the fuck up!

Tidir is looking at me. She knows there's no way out of this. She would volunteer if she believed the man in charge would listen to her. She's afraid he won't. She's afraid he'll do the opposite if we don't play by his rules. I would give my life without hesitation. I know she'll gladly give hers if it means saving our son, but I don't know if I can do it for her.

—Oh, I think you've made up your mind, Samaritan! I can see it in your face. You look like a man who's made a decision. All you have to do now is say the words.

She knows what I have to do, but it's too hard. I won't kill my wife.

—Tougher than you thought. I get that. I'll make you a deal, Samaritan. You don't need to say it. We both know what you chose. All you have to do is nod. Just nod and I'll do the rest.

Tidir is coming closer.

—Close your eyes, Ramzi.

She puts her hand on the window. I put my hand over

hers. She's looking at me with such tenderness, such calm. I want to trade places with her. I would give my life to save hers. I would give anything. But I will not watch my son die in front of me. Neither will she.

—*Ramzi. I said close your eyes. Put your hands over your ears and close your eyes. You too, Salma.*

—*All right, Samaritan. I'm going to count to three . . . ONE!*

—*Please, sir. Don't make me do—*

—*Yeah, yeah. I don't. I can't. Blah blah blah. We've been through this already. TWO!*

Tidir's eyes are tearing up, but she's smiling at me. I know she's scared. I know there's a part of her that wants to scream, and run, and fight. But she's not. She won't. She doesn't want our kids to see that. She wants to make this easier on them. She's also thinking of me. She knows part of me will die with her, but there has to be some part of me left for our children.

—*TH—*

I nod. I close my eyes.

TAK

NNNNOOOOOOOOOOOOOOOOOOOOOOO!!!

7.

DEEP SITS ALONE AT the desk and watches Idir scream and fall to his knees on the big screen in front of him. He smiles. He's proud of himself. He went where no one had gone before, boldly. That was science. He observed, theorized, then proved a hypothesis. Maximized group dynamics. He won't say it himself, but he'd like someone else to say his K3 was a work of art. He did it. He'll make Idir a citizen.

Laura storms back into the control room and turns on the lights.

—*Have you lost your* fucking mind?

—*What?*

She is followed by her own supervisor, a balding man in his fifties wearing a beige cardigan over his government-issued grey shirt. The balding man is Tom. He's been here since the very beginning. He was a tech when it all started, and now he's responsible for a small army of operators. He was once proud of that. He doesn't remember ever being as eager, as ambitious as Deep, but he was. Over the years his ambition has made way for an even stronger desire for comfort, peace, and quiet. All Tom really wants is for things to run smoothly. If it were up to him, no operator would ever quit or retire, and the program would never expand. All these things mean new people and new people mean . . .

—*You! What's your name?*

—*Deep.*

—*What you just did . . .*

Aside from a slew of medical issues—heartburn, high cholesterol, high blood pressure—Tom has some anger issues to deal with. He's doing his best to breathe in and breathe out, calling on every trick he's learned in group sessions.

—*What you just did . . . is* wrong.

—*What? What did I do? He passed K3!*

Deep rewinds the video to show Idir begging the terrorist to kill him. Tom is well aware of what transpired; he saw it from his office. But watching it again—Idir's son putting his hands over his ears, Idir's wife putting her hand on the window, the terrorist firing his gun—Tom realizes how much trouble they're all in. This isn't just highly irregular. It isn't just the kind of thing that gets people fired. This is the kind of thing that gets out. There have been mistakes in the past, plenty of them, but never anything this juicy. This . . . it's too good not to leak. It's a bloody piece of meat in shark-infested water. It'll get out. It's only a matter of when.

—*It's . . . his family, you gormless git!*

Tom regrets using those words. Deep is obviously an idiot, but that's no reason to be unprofessional. What matters now is containment.

—*So what? He passed!*

Tom no longer regrets using those words. He's getting agitated. He can see it all. A minister resigning. The Prime Minister denying everything. They'll find a patsy, or two, or three. Containment.

—*Laura, close the door. No one leaves this room.*

Laura gets up and locks everyone inside. Deep resets the big screen to a live view. Idir is on his knees, crying.

—*Guys! What's going on? He passed K3. He volunteered. He volunteered like . . . five times! He was willing to* die *right there and then! Did you see that?*

Tom's furious.

—*You. Stupid. Little. Shit. You can't use the man's family!*

—*He.* Passed*!*

—*You can't do that! You can't use his family!*

—*Why?*

—*Because . . . it's against the rules.*

—*No. It's not! You're talking about Appendix A, item number four. That doesn't apply!*

If Deep is guilty of anything, not knowing what's in the manual is not a part of it.

BRITISH VALUES ASSESSMENT—APPENDIX A—GENERAL HOSTAGE PARAMETERS.

4. Under no circumstances shall an operator use a person having any personal or professional connection with the subject as a candidate in a kill exercise. To do so would nullify the results.

Tom takes a deep breath.

—*Don't you think that, maybe, being his wife and kid qualifies as "having a connection"?*

—*Yeah, maybe. But it only talks about one! There's nothing in there about using two people he knows.*

Tom wonders how much more trouble he'd be in if he also beat some sense into this kid.

—*That's because they didn't think anyone would be stupid enough to ever do that, you . . .*

Pillock. Plonker. Prat. Tosser. Tom realizes he doesn't need to say the words out loud to get the satisfaction.

Deep still feels he should be congratulated, not scolded. He goes on to explain that item number four was, in his humble opinion, meant for all the other kills where the subject has to pick between two people. Obviously, in that situation, choosing between your best friend and someone you've never met wouldn't be much of a test. But K3 doesn't require choosing. It requires self-sacrifice, and Idir did that, several times. Deep's spirit-of-the-law speech doesn't seem to move Tom, or Laura, for that matter. Deep doesn't know Tom, but Laura . . . he thought Laura of all people would understand.

Deep is beginning to realize the depth of the hole he dug for himself. Tom grabs Deep's BVA manual from the desk and flips it to Appendix A.

—*How about this one? Did you think about this one?*

Item 11. Under no circumstances shall an operator create a minor as a candidate during a kill exercise.

—*Create! It says create. I used his real family.*

—*No you didn't! How do I know you didn't? Because none of it is real, you moron. None of them are! If they're in there, you made them. Now grab a pen and start filling out forms. We'll be here for a while. . . . You better hope that little stunt of yours doesn't land us all in jail.*

Jail? Deep doesn't understand.

—*What forms? We need to finish the test! He hasn't done K4 yet.*

Laura shakes her head.

—*You really don't get it, do you?*

—*No! I don't get it. He passed! . . . What kind of forms?*

—*There's the incident report. You'll need to explain what happened. I have to sign off on the test interruption.*

—What? He—

—He passed, I know. But it's over now. . . . Then we need authorization to erase this whole mess. They'll want to make sure this never happened. We need a warrant to wipe his memory without a failed test, another one for deportation.

—Stop. Stop. You just said this wasn't a failed test. I know I've said this before, but he passed K3. He did! You saw it! Don't punish him for a technicality. Don't . . . don't send his family away. Can't we just keep going? Finish the test?

—No. That's not possible anymore.

—Why?! He's here. He's doing it. He can do this.

—K3 doesn't count, Deep. You fucked it up. Even if it did, what are you going to do about K4?

—What do you mean?

—Imagine you just escaped the zombie apocalypse and watched all your friends being eaten alive. Now I'm asking you which fabric softener smells nicer.

It is just now dawning on Deep that no matter how clever his rendition of K3 may have been, he didn't anticipate the problems it might cause for Idir in K4. During the BVA, subjects are placed in traumatic situations. While government studies show that the vast majority of subjects recover completely given the right medication, most show symptoms of Acute Stress Disorder in the immediate aftermath, often *during* the test. ASD is similar to PTSD in many ways—patients suffering from the former will be diagnosed with the latter if the symptoms persist—but with a focus on dissociative symptoms. These include, but are not limited to, derealization and depersonalization—nothing around you feels real, not even your own thoughts or emotions. Detachment, emotional unresponsiveness, and a general feeling of numbness.

—*You're saying he won't make the right decision because of his dissociative symptoms?*

—*I'm saying he won't give a shit! It doesn't matter who or what you put in front of him. He won't care! This is a man who just watched his wife die! You made him kill his wife! Do you get that? Do you really think he'll care about the asshole or the single mother now? He can't continue.*

—*Is there any way to fix this?*

Tom emerges from the filing cabinet with a stack of paper in his hands.

—*What are you two talking about?*

—*Deep here wants us to finish the test.*

—*It's over, son.*

—*No, it's not! He can continue! He can!*

Tom looks for the score sheet on the desk but can't find it.

—*What did he get on the written test?*

Laura gets the score sheet from underneath Deep's manual.

—*He . . . he did question nine, but one of them he didn't*

know the answer to. We had to give it to him.

Tom whispers to himself. He's never been good with numbers and needs to do the math out loud.

—*Eight points won't do it, son. He needed K3 to pass. Even if he aced K4 now, which he won't do, that's not enough. Wipe him clean and put him on a plane.*

No one is noticing Idir on the large screen. He's pounding at the floor with both hands.

—*No! He passed! He's selfless, and courteous, and environmentally conscious. He passed!*

Deep is upset. He's not thinking about himself at this point. Surely he failed his own evaluation, but he wants to see Idir through this. He *needs* Idir to succeed. Guilt hasn't set in yet. What Deep is experiencing is just narcissistic identification and a very strong case of narrative transportation. At this point, Deep is incapable of separating Idir's success of failure from his own. He's so caught up in the simulation that his feelings and opinions are filtered through the rules of the game. He's seeing the world in BVA terms. Idir is environmentally conscious *because* he recycled the plastic wrapper. He's selfless because he chose the preferred option in K3. He's a good man because he has thirty-two points. Good men don't get put on the plane.

—*Can we give him another chance? Erase his memory and let him try again?*

Tom waits for Laura to answer.

—Can't do it.

—But the manual says it's completely safe.

—It is. It won't kill him. But I've put people on the plane, and it's not as pretty as what the brochure says. He'll forget everything that happened, that's for sure. He'll also forget he has a dog, or where he went to school. He might forget what he likes for breakfast, how much he loves his wife. He won't be the same man, and if he fails again . . . We do this to him twice and we'll turn him into a vegetable. I'm sorry.

—He won't fail! He hasn't failed! He passed!

—I know. I know. I wish there was something we could do, but there isn't. It's time to let go.

She turns off the monitor showing Idir in the hospital bed. She hands Deep his manual and his notebook. Deep picks them up and grabs his backpack from the floor. He gets up and walks away with his head down. He mumbles:

—He passed. . . .

Laura reaches forward to turn off the large screen. She pauses.

—Wait. Wait.

—What?

—Look!

8.

IDIR IS KNEELING ACROSS the window from his wife's body, his head against the floor. He's crying, whimpering, hitting the ground with his fist. He looks up at Tidir's lifeless body and starts pounding with both hands, screaming. The man in charge asks him to stop. Idir doesn't.

In the control room, Laura grabs the microphone.

—*I think he's losing it. We need him to calm down.*

Behind the glass wall, computer technicians are frantically typing instructions.

On the big screen, the man in charge knocks on the window with his fist.

—*Samaritan, you cut this shit right now. . . . Did you hear what I just said? Stop it now or I'm going to* really *hurt you.*

Idir is pounding harder and harder.

—*Now you've done it, Samaritan. What's your son's name? Do you want to make him an orphan? He's a little short on parents already.*

Idir doesn't stop. The man in charge nods at the terrorist in the test room and Idir gets the butt of an M-16 to the back of the head. He falls to the side but won't stay down. He shakes it off, touches the back of his head, and wipes the blood on his shirt.

Laura gets closer to the microphone, but Tom stops her.

—*No, no. Wait.*

Idir rushes the man standing over him. He grabs him by the legs and sends him to the ground. Idir is on top, punching as hard as he can. Blood gushes from the man's nose. Idir keeps hitting, screaming. He unleashes all his rage; fists keep raining down until the man's face is no longer a face. Idir gets up and grabs the weapon.

In the control room, everyone just stares. Even the technicians have abandoned their computer to watch.

Idir points the weapon at the man in charge and pulls the trigger. Nothing happens. He lowers the weapon to look at it, pushes and pulls the arming handle a few times. He tries firing again. Nothing. He looks at the weapon on both sides and finds the safety mechanism. He lets out a small sigh of relief, then the other four terrorists start firing at him.

Idir stands in the middle of the test room. Windows are exploding all around him. He gets hit in the leg, then the gut. A bullet tears through his chest. Another. And another.

Laura turns the small monitor back on. Idir's body is convulsing on the hospital bed. His heartbeat goes through the roof, then he flatlines. Nurses run to Idir's side and check his pupils. On the large screen, Idir drops to his knees, his body riddled with bullet holes. He tries to say something. Blood gushes from his mouth. He falls backwards.

The control room is silent, except for the heart monitor alarm. Laura is the first one to react.

—*He needs a doctor. Get the doctor in there!*

A nurse pushes a cart next to Idir's bed. A doctor walks in. The nurse cuts Idir's robe open. The doctor grabs the paddles from the cart and everyone stands clear. No change in pulse. The doctor hits him with another charge and Idir's body jumps. On the large screen, his bloodied corpse moves in unison.

Deep is squeezing Laura's arm hard, but she can't feel a thing.

—*Come on! Come on, friend! Live!*

One more electric shock. Idir's chest rises as he takes his first breath. Everyone looks at the heart monitor. They feel their own hearts slowing down to the regular beat of the machine. The doctor checks Idir's vitals, then gives a thumbs-up to the camera.

Deep looks at his hand on Laura's arm and lets go. She just now notices the pain. Deep puts his hand on her shoulder to get her attention.

—*He'll live?*

Sylvain Neuvel

—*Looks that way.*

Deep starts crying like a baby. Laura smiles at him.

—*Oh, don't cry. You know what that means, right?*

—*What?*

—*We have ourselves a hero!*

—*A . . . We do, don't we? Does that mean he . . . ?*

—*With flying colours.*

—*He passed?!*

—*He passed.*

Deep senses the weight of the world lifted off his shoulders. He doesn't feel the rush of victory—perhaps it's not his to feel—but a soothing sense of order. Idir's success strengthens Deep's faith in the universe, his belief in cosmic justice, his conviction that good always triumphs over evil.

—*This is control. You can start the awakening.*

Laura isn't easily moved. She's seen too much in her years as an operator. Yet she is surprised at how happy she feels—for Idir, yes, but mostly for Deep.

—*You should go down there.*

—*What?*

—*You should go.*

—*Can I?*

—*Yeah! Go! Go!*

Deep grabs his backpack and is about to leave the room. His thoughts turn to himself.

—*What about me? What's going to happen to me?*

—*We'll see. Either way, I think you should be the one to tell him.*

Deep smiles. His future is uncertain. He's proven himself unfit to be an operator, but this *is* the first time a subject has died during the BVA. They will want to study what happened, gather as much data as they can from Idir's simulation. They'll want to talk to Deep. They'll want to talk to Deep a lot. That might prove difficult if he's a disgruntled former trainee with an ironclad nondisclosure agreement. More than anything, they won't want any of this to get out. In the end, it might be better for everyone if Deep continues working here in some capacity. One thing is certain: he has earned himself a place in BVA history. The one whose hero died. Right now, none of it matters. There is only one thing in Deep's mind.

Idir is a citizen.

9.

MY NAME IS IDIR Jalil, and I'm a citizen.

I own a small dental practice in Bayswater. My wife, Tidir, is a journalist. She writes a weekly column in an online paper. We have two children, Ramzi and Salma. Both are doing very well in school. We are well liked by our neighbours, I think. My wife and I volunteer at the local charity shop. We are a typical middle-class family.

It was a year ago that I took the test for my family and earned us the right to stay. I remember everything about the test itself, every detail, down to the smells, but I have almost no memory of what came after. I remember dying—at least I thought I was dying. I woke up in a hospital bed. There were nurses, doctors. There was a young man trying to tell me things. I would not listen. All I wanted was to keep dying.

I do remember stepping back into the waiting room, seeing my wife, alive. I sobbed like a baby. I couldn't stop, didn't try to. I was . . . so happy to *see* her. The small wrinkles around her eyes. The pores of her skin. She felt undeniably real, and seeing her erased the lingering doubt

I had that this was still happening in my head. For a moment, a second or so, I felt like everything was going to be fine, that the dream was over and that our lives would go on as they had before. "So? How did it go?" she asked. I answered with a smile. Then she looked at me and I saw it. Pride. Her eyes were overflowing with it. I felt my soul turn to dust. She was proud of me.

I could not tell her. If anyone found out, we'd be stripped of our rights and sent back to the very place we ran from. Even in a world without consequence, this was not—*is* not—something I could ever share with her. She wouldn't understand. Or she would. That is the problem. She would say she doesn't blame me, that she'd have made the same choice if she were in my place. She would call me courageous, and she would mean all those things because it was all a simulation and none of it was real. It's easy to forgive something that didn't happen. But it did. I was there. I was there, and I told someone to shoot her in the head. Virtual or not, it *was* my reality. What I did, the choices I made . . . I did what I did and I chose what I chose. I did not pretend. The world around me might have been a fairy tale, but I was . . . me. Always me. They could not simulate that.

Every day I try to get better at living with myself. The pills they give me make the guilt bearable, and I take them religiously. If I am alone and absorbed in a book or a movie, I sometimes forget about it all. Tidir understands. She knows I keep something dark from her, but she did the same for us in Teheran and that makes it my right to return the favour. She wants to help in any way she can, but she doesn't understand that it is her presence I can't bear. I can't stand it. The pain, the guilt, her hand on the glass pane. I resent my wife for still loving me. I think less of her because she forgives what I can't. I think less of myself for feeling that way.

I do what I can to be pleasant, but there is a distance between us, a chasm I dare not traverse. I find things to do when she talks to me—I pick up after the kids, I do the dishes, anything to justify having my back to her. I have not looked her in the eye since the test. I avoid her gaze as best I can. I am afraid she will see right through me and realize what I am. I could not live with that.

There is a darkness in me, now. A monster awakened from a very long sleep. I suppose it was always there, but now it's running loose. I get angry at things, insignificant things. I snap at Tidir for being kind to me. I scold my children for being children. I choose my words carefully like I would a weapon. I hurt the people I love. I watch it all happen like I would a movie. I do not trust the man in the mirror anymore.

Six months ago over breakfast, Ramzi knocked his grape juice down on the kitchen table. I didn't get up.

I didn't put my newspaper down. I watched the purple shape reach the end of the table and drip onto my shoe. Then I hit him. I slapped him hard on the cheek. I felt the futility of regret when I saw fear in my daughter's eyes. She's seen the monster and she can't unsee it. What hurt me the most was the way Ramzi took it. He didn't cry. He found a cleaning cloth and wiped the juice off the table, then he looked at me, unsure if he should clean my shoe. It wasn't just a boy trying to make amends. I saw . . . respect. He'd learned something that morning, something horrible that would stay with him his whole life.

I wanted to leave—not the room, or the house, or the town. I thought the pills were the only thing keeping me here, so I stopped taking them for a week. I'm still here. I think about leaving from time to time. I wonder if anyone would miss me. I think about leaving, but I don't. I'm still here. I choose to stay. I stay because I'm a father. I will always love my children, and I will be there for them, to cherish them and protect them, even from me. I stay because I am a husband. Even in the darkness I carry, my wife still shines bright. She is the beacon I follow whenever I have doubts. I owe Tidir a life. It's a debt I can never repay, but the least I can do is try. I stay because I am a doctor, a neighbour, a friend. I stay because I have a responsibility to the people around me.

My name is Idir Jalil, and I'm a citizen.

Acknowledgments

I want to thank Lee Harris and everyone at Tor.com for giving this story a home. Thank you to my agent, Seth, and the amazing team at Gernert, and to Jon Cassir at CAA. To my son and all the kids who see people as people and haven't learned how to hate, thank you. You give me hope.

About the Author

James Andrew Rosen

SYLVAIN NEUVEL dropped out of high school at age fifteen. Along the way, he has been a journalist, worked in soil decontamination, sold ice cream in California, and peddled furniture across Canada. He received a PhD in linguistics from the University of Chicago. He taught linguistics in India and worked as a software engineer in Montreal. He is also a certified translator, though he wishes he were an astronaut. He likes to tinker, dabbles in robotics, and is somewhat obsessed with Halloween.

He absolutely loves toys; his girlfriend would have him believe that he has too many, so he writes about aliens and giant robots as a blatant excuse to build action figures (for his son, of course). He is the author of the Themis Files series: *Sleeping Giants* ("One of the most promising series kick-offs in recent memory"—NPR), *Waking Gods* ("In a word: unputdownable."—*Kirkus Reviews*), and *Only Human* ("Two [giant, robotic] thumbs up!"—*Kirkus Reviews*).

TOR·COM

Science fiction. Fantasy. The universe.

And related subjects.

*

More than just a publisher's website, *Tor.com*

is a venue for **original fiction, comics,** and

discussion of the entire field of SF and fantasy,

in all media and from all sources. Visit our site

today—and join the conversation yourself.

CPSIA information can be obtained
at www.ICGtesting.com
Printed in the USA
LVHW041816140319
610673LV00002B/208

9 781250 312839